Praise for *The Real Beauty*

Rave
Book
Reviews

"As divorce shatters the lives of children into broken pieces, *The Real Beauty* comes along like a careful application of loving glue. I wish I had had this book when my parents got divorced."

- Nicole Franco, Producer of the motion picture film
   "To Save a Life"

"*The Real Beauty* offers sound advice on how to navigate through the stages of grief as well as tools to handle a variety of emotional reactions. It certainly is refreshing to finally have a series of books in which amazing young writers collaborate with professionals to touch the young lives of others and provide awareness, guidance and even some certainty in uncertain times."

- Linda Shook Sorkin, MA, LMFT, licensed Marriage and
   Family Therapist and certified Teen Life Coach.
   soulempoweredcoaching.com

"Divorce is a very common, very real part of our everyday lives. We've all either been affected, or know someone who has been affected by divorce ... *The Real Beauty*, written by a child in terms that other children can understand, brings us encouragement and hope as we travel with young Brian Wallace through the chaotic emotions of divorce. The wonderful "Action Steps" and additional information included at the end of the book provide guidance and support for children and adults on similar journeys."

- Lewis Ribner, Ph.D., Clinical Psychologist

"This book helps to normalize the feelings of grief that happen in divorce and helps you to know that you are not alone. Wisdom written from the view point of a young adolescent, as in *The Real Beauty*, will help their peers through the process, loss, change, and effects of divorce. It gives the reader someone to relate to, identify with, and move toward healing."

- Karen Clark, San Diego Rescue Mission and Marriage and Family Therapist Trainee

"As an educator, I appreciate materials that teach students real-life coping tools. There are not many resources out there that cover such realistic issues from a child's point of view. *The Real Beauty* is an all encompassing tool and even teaches vocabulary through-out the book."

- Michelle Brashears, 6th grade teacher - Del Mar Union School District

"This book is an important and beautiful story depicting a journey of learning and healing from a child's perspective. Children who read this book will find solace, comfort, and affirmation. More importantly, parents who are in the process of divorce will find insightful and illuminating information regarding the emotional impact of a very trying time in a child's life. Additionally, the practical and helpful recommendations and exercises offered at the end of the book will undoubtedly be of great use to those who are humble enough to realize that they will need all the help that they can get in negotiating the tough experience of divorce. Lastly, from a school psychologist perspective, parents would be wise to consider the academic and social impact of divorce all too often observed within the school setting. Children going through a divorce, who are humble enough to recognize and deal with the emotional fallout from divorce will benefit emotionally, socially, and academically from using this book."

- Richard Griswold, Ph.D - School Psychologist AF/SC

THE
REAL BEAUTY

ILLUSTRATED BY

KIANA ARYAN

WRITTEN BY

KATHRYN MOHR

DEDICATIONS:

To my family, for encouraging
me to be my best.
—Kathryn Mohr

To Mom & T.E.A.M.
—Kiana Aryan

In loving memory of my father,
John Edward Merryman
—Kristyn Braund

To those men who "stood in the gap," my
Mom who made sacrifices, and the many
kids and families at Forest Home and
Solana Beach Presbyterian Church who
allow me to share my story with them.
—Billy Jack Blankenship

To my husband and children and to my parents
Jerry and Rosalie M. Carter who dedicated
their lives to creating The Electronic Bookshelf
(now Scholastic Reading Counts!) to help
children around the world to motivate
and teach them to read.
—Colleen C. Ster

CHARITY:
A portion of sales from this book will be
donated to the American Lung Association
in memory of John Edward Merryman

SALES:
The student author and illustrator of this book
will be distributing a portion of their earnings
into their college savings funds.

4114U: How to Read and Use this Book

Dear Reader,

You may be reading this story for pleasure, or you may have chosen this book because you can relate to its subject matter. Either way, here are some helpful instructions to navigate and guide your way through this book:

1. Read and enjoy the story, notice the vocabulary footnotes, and also remember the story was written and illustrated by kids just like you. If your own family has been going through the divorce of your parents, or if you are moving or experiencing some other life-changing event, ask yourself if the characters in this story demonstrate some of the same emotions or feelings that you have been experiencing.

2. After you read the story, you will find a section called 4114U. This section has been put together by experts to give you some helpful tips and advice on how to work through your parents' divorce or other significant events in your life. You will find activities to do by yourself, as well as some healing activities to do with a parent or loved one.

3. Because true healing requires you to focus on your emotional, educational, social, and even spiritual needs, we have divided the 4114U portion of the book into the following three sections:

- Action Steps to Help Kids Emotionally
- Action Steps to Help Families Socially
- Action Steps to Help Families Spiritually

One of our goals is that you will feel like this book was written just for you. We want you to see that others struggle with life altering events just like the one you are experiencing. We also want to give you some hope that things are going to get better and empower you (and your parents) with the necessary tools to assist you in dealing with divorce, moving, or any life challenge that may come your way.

While we hope you find this book helpful, please keep in mind that its content is not meant to be a substitute for any professional medical advice, diagnosis, or treatment. We hope you enjoy this book.

All the best,

Colleen C. Oster

President/Publisher, Reflections Publishing

Published by Reflections Publishing
© 2010 Reflections Publishing

This book is a work of fiction. Names, characters, businesses, organizations, places, events, and incidents either are the product of the author's imagination or are used fictitiously. Any resemblance to actual persons, living or dead, events, or locales is entirely coincidental.

First Edition. Published in the United States of America.

ISBN 978-1-61660-000-6

Visit our website at www.reflectionspublishing.com for more information or inquiries.

Chapter 1:
A World Unraveling

Brian Wallace closed his suitcase and sighed. He stood up and looked around his bare room; then he walked to the far side of the room, sat on one of the moving boxes, and looked out his apartment window. He tried to look up at the colossal[1] skyscrapers of New York City instead of down at the orange moving truck with boxes being loaded into it.

Brian's thoughts drifted to how drastically his life had changed during the last year. Once upon a time, Brian's parents were happy living in their quaint[2] apartment; that was a long time ago though, and Brian now struggled to remember any of those happy moments. Instead, he focused on the thorny mess his family's lives had become—a mess no box could hold.

At first ... initially, Brian's father

---

[1] colossal: huge, gigantic, massive in size
[2] quaint: cute, attractive, small, old-fashioned style

easily became irritated by even the tiniest of inconveniences. Eventually, he formed a habit of disappearing early each night to the solitude of his study. Brian's mother, Mum, had also become quite good at avoiding the obvious, at least for awhile. His parents seemed to just pass each other throughout the day. They coexisted[3] at home on the weekends and tried to be polite to each other at night during the weekdays. Their only interaction was at dinner when they attempted to put on happy faces for Brian and his sister. In the end, requests to pass the butter simply did not provide much in the way of real communication.

[3] coexisted: to exist and live at the same time and place

Brian was not exactly sure what happened between his parents. Most of the reasons were simply beyond Brian's comprehension.[4] Instead, Brian blamed himself. He must have done something. If only he could figure out what had gone wrong, then he could try to fix it.

Ultimately, the silence in the house became simply unbearable[5] for Brian's parents. Eventually, his mother was the first to crack. One day, Brian's mother decided life was too short to be miserable for the rest of her life. With her family life unraveling in New York City, she packed a suitcase and announced she was going to visit her parents in Wisconsin. Initially, she had intended to go away

[4] comprehension: understanding
[5] unbearable: intolerable, impossible to deal with

for only a few days—just a quick trip to check on her aging mother and father to make sure they were doing okay; that was what she said at least.

At the time, Brian's mother was very well-intentioned.[6] She thought being back in the country, in her old hometown, would clear her head and help her find a solution to her marital[7] problems. Instead, during her stay, she ran into her old high school sweetheart. He had recently lost his wife to cancer. They innocently chatted over a cup of coffee. Then, she extended her trip to a week. One week became two, and soon after, the trip was extended indefinitely.[8]

When she eventually went back to

[6] well-intentioned: trying to help, but sometimes causes a bad result
[7] marital: relating to someone who got married in a wedding
[8] indefinitely: no ending time has been set

New York, Brian's mother asked his father for a quick, painless divorce.[9] She explained to him that she thought trying to work things out would only fail because she just couldn't go back to living a loveless life. His father's indifference[10] didn't help matters; instead it solidified[11] his mother's thinking that she was making the right decision. Brian's parents' marriage quickly came to an end.

Things hastily[12] spiraled[13] down from there. His mother and father were divorced within months. Then, his mother almost immediately eloped with her high school sweetheart, Dale Smith.

Brian was amazed at how quickly his life had become unpredictable.[14]

[9] divorce: when parents split up and are not legally married anymore
[10] indifference: not interested or concerned
[11] solidified: to set or harden one's thinking
[12] hastily: very fast or quickly
[13] spiraled: when a situation takes a turn for the worse
[14] unpredictable: not knowing what is coming next

Brian's feelings of guilt increased. He began to believe that he and his younger sister, Carla, must have been the reason for his parents' struggle to keep the family together.

Some of his friend's parents were divorced. He had noticed that Brian's friends had confided that—at some point—they felt responsible for their parents getting divorced. This made Brian wonder: if he had just gone to bed on time, kept his room cleaner, been a stronger student, been nicer to his sister, if … if … if … then maybe, just maybe, his parents would have been able to work things out.

Did the stress of having children

put them over the edge? Brian kept wondering how adults could have kids yet not attempt to stay together as a family. Things were never going to be the same ever again.

Furthermore, he was not even sure what a normal day was going to be now, especially since his parents came to the solution that he would move to Wisconsin with his mother, while Carla would stay put in New York City with their father. Brian wondered how splitting the family apart could be considered any kind of solution at all.

Chapter 2:
The Move

Brian was sitting, lost in thought, when suddenly the door opened. Two big, burly men in overalls, with cigars hanging out of their mouths, shuffled into his childhood room.

"Outta the way, kid! We don't wanna drop anything on ya," growled one of the movers. Brian didn't want to give these grumpy men another excuse to yell at him, so he hurried out and closed the door. It was about time to leave anyway, and he needed to meet Mum in the lobby. But first, he walked down the narrow hall to Dad's study and knocked on the closed door.

"Password?" Dad asked.

Brian felt an anger bubble growing inside him. This was the last day Dad would see him and Mum for a long time and he still needed the password?

"Adaperio," he said. Adaperio is

Latin for open. Dad, he thought, was obsessed[15] with a dead language.

"Yes indeed, it is open. Come in," said Dad. He was working at his desk, as always.

Brian looked around the study. The shelves housed old, dusty books that were going to fall apart any minute, as well as, two stiff wooden reading chairs. It also had one small desk lamp that, when turned on at night, made the room simply gloomy.

"Why can't Mum and I stay here?" Brian burst out.

Dad hesitated, then responded, "I know that separating you and your sister is not an ideal solution, but this is the best

[15] obsessed: to worry or think about something all of the time

arrangement[16] that your mother and I could come up with for now. We finally got Carla into the special needs program, and Mum and I don't want her to lose her spot. Things can always change though, you know."

Life is not fair, Brian thought. *It's just not fair that Carla and Dad get to stay in New York while we have to move to some tiny, dumb town in Wisconsin.*

His dad turned to focus back on his work, then added distractedly,[17] "Well, this is it. Take care of your mother, Brian. Things will work out for the best." Brian began to leave, but stopped when Dad said, "Brian—I will miss you. Do well in school and come to visit us. I know you will be seeing New York

[16] arrangement: agreed, organized plan
[17] distractedly: anxious and not able to focus or think clearly

again very soon. Please e-mail me. You know I check it every day for my work." Then, Brian's father rose to hug Brian, and Brian tentatively[18] hugged him back, unsure of what or how to feel. He knew his father was trying and that he meant well, however, Brian knew his dad was better at working from dawn until dusk every day than at showing emotion.

As soon as Brian returned downstairs, his mother exclaimed, "Oh, good —there you are. It's time to get in the car. The movers are ready," she said.

They went down the elevator to say goodbye to Carla, who had been waiting in the lobby because she found it too painful to watch the movers tear their lives apart box by box.

[18] tentatively: hesitant with no certainty

After all the hugs and kisses, Brian and Mum walked out to the car. The movers signaled that they were ready, then Mum pulled her keys out and silently drove away from the apartment building—the only home Brian had ever known.

As they exited town, he looked up, trying to see the top of every building in sight for the last time. He knew he was going to miss it. He thought … *Sure, the country doesn't have the pollution, but it also doesn't have 1,400 feet tall buildings everywhere either. Sure the country has open plains, but in the city those open plains are filled with stores and restaurants of every type. How could a small town ever compare to the humongous[19] city of New York?*

[19] humongous: enormous, immense, super big, vast

Chapter 3:
A New Life

During the trip, Brian finally realized, *Oh, my gosh! I forgot that I have a new stepdad and stepsister to meet.* He started to think about his new stepdad and stepsister, Dale and Zoe. A million and one questions began running through his mind as he thought about this new life that he was about to begin in Wisconsin.

Would his stepdad be crazy about work and Latin like his dad? Would he be the type that wants Mum to do all the cooking and housework? Would his stepdad have time for him? What about Zoe? She was 14 years old and he was 12! Carla was only eight. Would Zoe bully him and take his things like the big sisters in the TV shows? Do they have pets? What kind of accent do they have? Do they dress weird? Is their house big or small? All of these questions buzzed through his mind like a swarm of bees.

"You are awfully quiet back there, Sport," said Mum, "what is buzzing around in your head right now?"

"Nothing important," Brian lied.

They drove all the way to Ohio, stopping only for gas and food. Mum had reserved a room for them in a motel. When they got there and turned on the light, the sight of the room disgusted them. There were spider webs everywhere, the ugly brown paint was chipping off the wall, and in the corner, there were two, rugged beds covered in wool blankets. In the next room, the bathroom defied[20] description and the smell was rancid.[a]

---

[20] defied: to rebel or go against what is normal
[21] rancid: awful, foul smell

"Well," said Mum, "it will have to do. It's far too late to get a new room."

After they checked the pillows and blankets for spiders, Mum turned off the light. Brian fell into an uncomfortable and light sleep, he kept thinking that he felt something crawling on him.

In the morning, they packed quickly and drove away from that horrible motel as fast as possible. They made it to their new home in Wisconsin before midnight. Brian was disappointed that he could not see what the house looked like on the outside or any of the things surrounding it. All he could make out was a wooden fence.

With a knock on the door, a heavy

voice from inside the dark house said, "Come in!" Once inside the house, they saw a man sitting on a couch with a black and white cocker spaniel by his side.

"Ahhh, so you must be Liza and Brian. I am Dale Smith, for those of you who don't know," he said, winking at Brian jokingly.

Brian began to say, "We already know," but Mum very quickly beat him to the punch.

She ran up to Dale, gave him a big hug and kiss and exclaimed, "I can't believe this is really happening and we are in Wisconsin! I can't wait for you and Brian to get to know each other, so we can all have a fresh start together."

For Brian, it was so strange to see his mother hugging and loving someone other than his dad, and it must have been apparent.[22]

"Well," Dale said, seeing Brian's face, "I think it is time for the kiddos to head to bed."

Dale walked them up the hall to see Brian's new room, where there was only a sleeping bag.

"Sorry," said Dale. "We have been so busy working that we didn't get the bed moved up from the basement. I hope this will be okay for tonight."

"It's perfect," said Mum quickly trying not to make Dale feel badly.

Yeah, just perfect, Brian thought

[22] apparent: obvious, easy to see

bitterly to himself.

Suddenly, the dog started barking and Dale briskly walked back down the hall shouting, "Shush, Polly!"

Brian crawled into his sleeping bag, and Mum gave him a big hug and kiss good night. As she walked out of the room, she turned and said, "Thank you for coming with me, for doing this with me. I know this has been a hard couple of days, but please just give Dale a chance ... give me a chance to be happy again." She then closed the door and left.

Brian couldn't muster[23] the strength to give her a response.

---

[23] muster: to get the courage to do something

Chapter 4:
Meeting Misty

Around 6 A.M., Brian awoke to the sound of a slamming door. Curious, he crawled out of his warm, cozy sleeping bag and went outside.

It was a warm, July morning. Brian was glad to feel the warmth because he had heard that Wisconsin could be cold in July. He looked around the large farm and saw a white, painted, wooden fence surrounding the rolling pastures [24] filled with animals. Mostly sheep grazed, [25] but in the far field one horse was being led into the huge barn. He decided to follow the horse and the figure. The barn smelled of horse manure and fresh hay; inside he saw three horses. He did not notice the person hitching up the horse to a hook on the wall until he heard someone say, "Hi there!"

Startled, Brian turned and saw a

[24] pastures: a large field full of grass for cows, sheep, and horses
[25] grazing: to eat grass that is growing

girl who was grooming the horse. She was tall and skinny with red hair, brown eyes and very pale, freckled skin. She had a smile on her face.

"Hi," he said.

"Hi, I'm Zoe," she replied. "You must be the infamous[26] Brian," said Zoe jokingly.

"Mmmhmm," he mumbled, walking towards the horse.

"What's his name?" Brian asked.

"*Her* name is Bee."

The name fit the horse. She was pale yellow everywhere, except for on her face where there was a white patch.

"Can I help brush her?" he asked.

"Not wearing pajamas, you can't! Go

---

[26] infamous: being known for doing something bad

get changed and then come back," she said, laughing.

Brian blushed in embarrassment then trudged[27] out of the barn.

Brian changed into an old T-shirt and jeans and hurried back to the barn. Zoe had already put Bee away, and was now brushing a horse with a full, thick, brown coat.

"This one is Muddy," she said.

"He looks pretty clean to me," said Brian.

"No, *her* name is Muddy," said Zoe.

"Can I help you now?" Brian asked.

"Sure, just grab the curry comb."

"The what?" he asked.

"You have never done this?" Zoe

---

[27] trudged: to take long, slow, and heavy steps

asked surprised.

"Well, no, I lived in New York City and there aren't a lot of horses there," Brian answered shyly.

"Oh sure, then let me show you all of the brushes. This is the curry comb, the mane comb, the hoof pick, the dandy brush, the body brush, the water brush, and hoof oil."

Brian listened to Zoe very carefully, memorizing each one, when suddenly a brown and white splattered horse in the stall next to where he was standing caught his eye.

"There are numerous brushes to use while grooming a horse, but these are the basics," Zoe finished.

"Which horse is that?" asked Brian, pointing to the brown and white horse.

"Oh, her? She just came in. We got her from a man who has horses from the Chincoteague Island, and he wants to sell most of them so he can retire. He sold her pretty cheap for a horse, so we bought her after we found out you and your mom were coming. We call her Misty because she looks exactly like the horse in the book *Misty of Chincoteague*,[28] don't you think so?" asked Zoe.

"Sure," Brian said, even though he had never read the book.

"Can we brush Misty next?"

"No. Dad handles her because

[28] *Misty of Chincoteague* was written by American author Marguerite Henry in 1947. This true story is based on a Chincoteague Pony named Misty that lives on the coastal island of Chincoteague, Virginia. This book received a Newbery Honor award.

she's still a little jumpy and restless. After we put Muddy away and groom my horse, Kit-Kat, we can feed her with the others," Zoe said.

"Okay," said Brian.

So, they put Muddy away and then groomed Kit-Kat. Then it was time to feed the horses.

The last stall they walked to was Misty's. Zoe carefully approached her stall while talking to her in a soothing tone. She undid the latch to Misty's stall and Misty nickered nervously.

Zoe quickly filled her bucket with grain, refilled her water, and then said to Brian, "Can you please get some hay from that pile over there?"

Brian ran over and tossed some hay in the stall. Scared, Misty retreated to the back of her stall, neighing to the other horses as if to say to them, "Help! I'm being attacked here."

When Zoe was finished, she ran out and latched the stall, leaned against the wall. "She's much better than last week. I couldn't go near her or she would bite my hair."

Two hours had passed when they finally left the barn.

As they walked back to the house, Brian studied its features. The house was whitewashed with curtains in every window. There was an archway that led a path up to the house, and sunflowers bordered the front, some standing as tall as he was.

Back inside the house, Zoe showed Brian to the kitchen where Mum and Dale were eating breakfast.

"Morning," said Dale, "I see you two have met."

"Yep—he helped me groom some of our horses," said Zoe, pouring herself some juice.

"Did he now? Well, Sonny, did you know that you get to choose one of those horses to be your very own?" Dale asked.

"No, sir," said Brian.

"No, sir? Who is that? Around here we don't have any sirs. Just Dad."

"Is Dale okay?" Brian asked.

"Sure," said Dale looking more than slightly disappointed.

Brian studied his stepdad. He had a weathered[29] face, but he still looked jolly. He sported worn-out jeans, a plain white T-shirt, a cowboy hat, and boots which completed his cowboy style. Brian almost laughed when he realized how much of a difference existed between Dale and his Mum.

His mother wore a stylish red and white striped shirt with tailored,[30] tan capri pants. She did not have a wrinkle on her face, and looked very tired. Mum was not a morning person. She hated getting up early.

Brian started to sit down, but

[29] weathered: when something wears down over time and looks old
[30] tailored: custom-made, fitted, made-to-order

before he could take a bite, Dale stopped him and said, "Whoa there! You need a shower before you eat. Then, after breakfast, you and Liza can pick out your horses."

"I have one, too?" said Mum. "Oh, Dale, I can't ride a horse. My body won't take it …" she said, her voice fading off.

Zoe showed Brian to the bathroom. "Don't you dare use up all the hot water," she warned.

Brian scurried back to his room to grab clothes. Then, he took the fastest shower he had ever taken in his life.

He walked out dressed and Zoe said, "Wow, you're fast! I was only teasing."

Brian went to the kitchen for breakfast and ate quickly, wondering which horse was going to be his to ride.

After he was done, it seemed as if everyone else was eating in slow motion. He forced himself to wait quietly, trying not to look too eager. Finally, after putting on their shoes, everyone was ready. They walked to the barn where Brian noticed a sign that read, *8 Maples Farm*. Looking around, he began to spot maple trees all around the barn. There were two in the front and two on the sides, so he figured that there were also two in the back. When they finally reached the barn, Dale went into one of the empty stalls and came back with two halters.

Brian walked over to Zoe and whispered, "What are those?"

"They're called halters. They're like bridles, but they are more comfortable because there isn't a bit."

"What's a bit?" Brian asked.

"A bit is the metal piece that goes into the horse's mouth," said Zoe. "It helps riders control when they stop, go, turn, and change speeds."

After looking at the horses, Brian's Mum said, "Brian, you can choose first,"

While Brian was talking, Dale had brought out Bee and Misty. "These are the horses you can choose from, but if you want a smooth ride, then I would recommend Bee. She is less, um, rowdy than Misty," said Dale.

"I choose Misty," Brian said firmly.

"Are you sure, Sonny? Misty can be a bit of a handful, and you won't be able to ride her until she gets settled down in her new home," Dale said.

"I'm sure," said Brian in the same firm tone of voice.

"Well, Liza, then you get Bee, the sweetie pie!"

"Okay, Dale," Mum said.

Dale put the horses back in their stalls and said to Zoe, "Why don't you kids grab a couple of bikes and ride to town to look around?"

"Okay," Zoe said.

Brian felt his stomach lurch.[31] He

---

[31] lurch: when your stomach feels like it jerks and rolls around

had completely forgotten that Zoe was his stepsister now. He thought of Dad and Carla. He had missed them a lot last night, but in all of this excitement he had almost forgotten they even existed and this made him feel bad. All of a sudden, he did not feel like going to town.

Being away from his dad and Carla often hit him in waves of grief[32] which made it difficult to breathe at times.

His mind wandered back to the car ride from New York to Wisconsin. He began replaying saying good-bye to his dad and Carla. Tears began to well up in his eyes.

Embarrassed by this wave of emotion, Brian quickly wiped his tears away

---

[32] grief: overcome with sadness when something happens

before Zoe saw him.

"Um, maybe another time. I would really like to unpack my things now," he said.

"Okay, I'll get Zoe and your mom to help me carry your double-sized bed up from the basement."

"Her name is Mum not Mom!" Brian reacted angrily.

"Oh, I'm sorry," said Dale looking a little hurt. He started to walk away.

"Wait, I'm sorry," said Brian quietly, but Dale was already out of earshot.

As soon as Brian got back to the house, he went to his room to put his clothes in the closet. When he opened the closet doors, he saw a laundry basket and a few old books like *Tom Sawyer* and *Treasure Island*. He had just finished getting his clothes together and was putting everything away when he heard the scraping of bedposts against the wooden flooring. He ran out to see his new bed. It was not much, but it was better than he had expected. Mum and Dale lifted the double-sized headboard while Zoe followed with two, red, fluffy pillows and a picnic-blanket-checked bedspread.

"It's cool," he said.

"Hey, come help. I'm about to drop the pillows," said Zoe.

Brian helped to shove the headboard through his door and into the corner where he wanted it placed.

"If you want, we can get you a new bedspread …" began Dale.

"No, I like this just fine," said Brian.

Well, the movers should be here tomorrow with our things," said Mum.

The rest of the day was pretty un-eventful. The only fun part of the day was when Dale took Brian to the barn to show him how to ride Bee and how to groom Misty without upsetting her.

"It used to be Zoe's responsibility to groom all the horses except Misty. Now that your Mom, I mean your Mum, doesn't want the responsibility of Bee, it's now your responsibility to groom, feed, and exercise both horses.

---

[33] precautions: what you need to do to keep something bad from happening

You will need to take precautions[33] with Misty though until we can get her settled down. Does that sound okay with you?"

"Yeah, that'd be awesome Dale."

"Now, Zoe will help you with anything you feel uncomfortable with, and I can help you too, if Zoe is not around," said Dale. "We'll make a rider of you yet. I have a strong feeling you will do well."

After Dale's thorough explanations and a quick riding lesson, Brian walked back to the house. His head was still buzzing with all of Dale's instructions: Misty's rowdy, so be careful; she needs to be fed twice a day; this is how you put the saddle and bridle on; mount the horse like this; exercise her once a day for an hour; when exercising, you can ride Bee and put this long rope on Misty's halter, and run her around in that pasture over there. *I can't wait to start*, Brian thought to himself.

When he went back to the house, he finally got a tour of the entire inside. Zoe's room was down in the basement, Mum and Dale's room was down the hall on the left, and the bathroom was on the right. The family room was a cozy room in the center of the house just next to the kitchen.

It was now time for Brian to start his bedtime ritual, so he brushed his teeth, pulled on his pajamas, crawled into bed to read a bit, and then set his old alarm clock to 6 A.M. to get up the next morning.

Chapter 5:
Getting Spooked

The next morning came too quickly. *BBBBZZZZZ! BBBBZZZZZ!* Brian whacked his alarm clock and got up and got dressed rapidly. He wanted to beat

Zoe to the barn so he could have some time alone with Misty; he also wanted to see what she was like when it was just boy and horse.

It was a chilly morning, so Brian grabbed his fleece jacket on the way out. As he ran outside, it started to barely drizzle. *No outside exercise today*, he thought, as he ran to the barn.

When he got inside the barn, he was greeted by a nickering[34] sound.

"Morning," said Zoe, "is it raining out?" she asked.

"Yeah," he said as he unlatched Misty's stall.

"I want you to groom Bee first, to get the hang of everything," she said.

---

[34] nickering: slang term for horses neighing

"Fine," he mumbled back.

Bee's halter was already on, so Brian led her straight to another set of hooks behind Kit-Kat's stall. He hooked her up, then went into the room where Dale had gotten the halters the day before. He grabbed the grooming box and hauled it out to Bee's hook. First, he started with the curry comb, then used the body brush, and lastly, finished with the hoof pick. Then, Zoe showed him where the grain, hay, and water could be found. He fed Bee before leading her back to her stall.

Brian felt his heart speed up. It was finally time! It was time to groom Misty. He could not wait to stroke her beautiful coat and soothe her like Dale and Zoe could do. He led her out of the stall to her hook just as the rain began to patter harder on the rooftop. He went through the same routine as with Bee, stroking and soothing all along her side. Then, he came to his last brush, the hoof pick. Just one more brush, and he would prove that he was capable of handling an almost-wild horse. He walked around to the back of Misty to clean her back hooves. When he bent over to pick the dirt out of her hoof, an enormous clap of thunder suddenly shook the entire barn.

The next few moments happened in slow motion. Misty neighed and Brian looked up from a kneeling position. Misty began to buck and Zoe screamed. Brian stood up to move away just too late and Misty's hoof hit his face, thrusting him against the wall. The last thing he saw was Zoe running out the door shouting, "Dad!" He heard a final neigh, a last boom of thunder, and then everything went black.

Chapter 6:
A Trip to the Hospital

That afternoon when the pain medication wore off, Brian finally opened his eyes. He sat up in the hospital bed and shouted, "AAHHHH!" His entire head hurt tremendously,[35] so he eased himself gently back down. "Where am I? Why am I in this strange place?" he asked. He found himself in a room that was small and white, with technical equipment all around. He then looked down at himself and saw that he was in a sterile hospital bed dressed in a blue, flimsy gown. He suddenly realized he was a patient in a hospital.

Next to him hung a tiny string that read, "Call for the Nurse." He pulled the string, and seconds later a nurse came in to check on him.

"Oh, why hello, Brian. Just one second." She ran outside the hall and shouted, "Dr. Estill! Brian is awake!"

---

[35] tremendously: huge, powerful

She went back into his room. "Sorry, about that, but there are some people here that will be glad to see you awake."

Brian had just enough time to wonder who Dr. Estill was before it all came surging back. He remembered the thunder, the bucking, and Zoe shouting. Then, he remembered that he had been kicked in the face. He lifted his hand to the area where he remembered being struck. A fairly big bump protruded from his forehead. The next thing he knew, someone else entered his room. He was guessing it was Dr. Estill.

"Hello, Brian. Do you know who I am?"

"I think you are Dr. Estill."

"Yes, you're right, but do you know who this is?" He waved in Zoe.

"Zoe," he said.

"Yes, good!" Dr. Estill continued to question Brian. "Who is this?" Dr. Estill waved to Mum.

"My Mum," he said.

"And who is this?" as he waved in Dale.

"My stepdad," he said.

"Good, no memory loss Brian. You had a serious concussion[36] from being kicked by a horse, but you should be all right. I'll leave you alone for a few minutes," said Dr. Estill.

"Oh, Brian, we were so scared. Are you okay?" asked Mum.

---

[36] concussion: when you have hit your head and lost consciousness

"How do you feel?" asked Dale.

Brian felt the color in his face rise and his face scowl.[37] All the anger he had been keeping inside began to boil right over.

"How do I feel? I feel terrible. I would not have a concussion and a huge headache if we had stayed in New York City. I wouldn't have had to move here if Mum had not divorced my real dad," Brian shouted. "But instead, I was dragged to a tiny town in the middle of nowhere that no one cares about or knows about."

"Brian!" said Mum sadly. "I'm ... we are sorry you are unhappy ... it is hard, I know ... well, Dale ... I think we

---

[37] scowl: to look at someone in an unhappy or angry way

should let Brian calm down a bit and go call his father to let him know that Brian is awake now. Brian, we'll see you in a little while. Are you coming, Dale?"

"Yes, Liza," and they left looking back at Brian sadly.

"Brian," started Zoe.

"Just leave me alone!" said Brian angrily, feeling very distraught.[38]

Zoe ran out following her parents.

The nurse walked in having seen Zoe run out upset and told Brian to try to rest for awhile.

"How long am I staying?" he asked the nurse impatiently.

"Probably two more nights," said the nurse.

[38] distraught: to be so upset that you stop thinking clearly

"Two more nights!" It seemed like that would be forever.

The nurse continued, "Just until we are sure it's safe for you to go home. We just do not want you to slip into a coma on us. However, you may watch television to pass the time, or I can bring you a movie if you like. Is there one you would like to watch?"

"Well," Brian asked calming down, "Do you have *Indiana Jones*?"

"I think we do. I will go find out —just give me a minute."

In the time the nurse was gone, Brian began feeling drowsy. He began looking around the room. He noticed that the bathroom was adjacent[39] to his

---

[39] adjacent: when an object or thing is next to something

bed and there was a small television set with a black screen. In the bathroom, Brian saw a mirror and stepped forward to see the spot where he had felt the bump. It was large and disgusting, and he screamed so loudly that a nearby nurse rushed in to ask what was wrong. She reassured[40] him that his injury would look better soon and walked out.

His nurse came back later with *Indiana Jones* in her hand. She slid it into the DVD player, but even before it began, Brian fell into a deep sleep. His Mum and Dale returned to his room and waited until visiting hours were over, but Brian continued to sleep through the night without knowing they were there.

---

[40] reassured: to make someone feel better or calmer

In the morning, he woke up and really stretched. He could hear birds chirping outside his window, the sun was shining and all felt peaceful. He felt like he was in a scenic movie, and the crisis had passed.

However, he soon became troubled when he remembered what happened the day before, realizing how stupid he had been. If he had just chosen Bee, he would not be in this mess. It was his fault, and he had hurt the feelings of his Mum, stepdad, and stepsister.

All of Brian's sad, forlorn,[41] and emotional thoughts were interrupted when the nurse came in and told him that his Mum and stepdad had waited

[41] forlorn: to be lonely, sad, or unhappy

patiently for him to wake up last night, but had finally gone home. They would be back later that day, but they first had to meet the movers who were delivering their stuff from New York.

The nurse asked Brian if he felt well enough to have breakfast in the hospital cafeteria instead of eating in his bed. She said she would be willing to show him the way and knew that there was another boy from down the hall who had just left to get something to eat.

"Sure," said Brian, and they headed to the cafeteria. There were dozens of people there, a few adults and a ton of kids. *It just goes to show you how careful we kids are,* Brian thought sarcastically.[42]

---

[42] sarcastically: to say the opposite of what you mean to show you are annoyed

Brian grabbed a tray, a bowl of cereal, and a banana. The nurse directed him to a table with a boy that appeared to be around Brian's age.

"Brian, I would like to introduce you to Bob. Bob, this is Brian," said the nurse.

After she introduced them to each other, she went back to her station.

"Hi," Bob said.

"Hi," replied Brian.

"What happened to you?" Bob inquired[43] curiously.

Brian swallowed a big mouthful of banana and told him, "A concussion. I got kicked by a horse."

"Ohhhh!, that must have hurt."

---

[43] inquired: to question to get information

Then he added, "My appendix [44] had to be removed. I go home today."

"Lucky! I mean that you get to leave today. I still have another night left."

"Where do you live?" asked Bob.

"I live on *8 Maples Farm*, but I just moved here from New York City."

Bob's eyes widened. "Wow, I'm jealous. I have lived here my entire life."

It was as if something had clicked. Instantly, Bob and Brian discussed where they lived, what bands they liked, and their favorite pets. Then, they found out they were in the same grade and going to the same school in the fall.

When they returned to their rooms, they asked the nurse if they could

[44] appendix: a small organ near your bowels where solid waste leaves your body

watch *Indiana Jones* in Brian's room. The nurse put the disc in the DVD player and pressed play. The boys had a great time watching the movie, pretending to shoot each other and swing on vines. Before they knew it, most of the day had slipped by, and Bob's parents came to pick him up. Before they said their goodbyes, they promised to stay really good friends.

Brian had never had a real friend. Carla had always been hard to talk to, and he was shy at his huge school in New York, so he did not hang out with many kids his own age.

After Bob left, Mum, Dale, and Zoe came to visit. Mum and Dale stayed quiet and Zoe would not even look at him at first. But Dale brought

Brian a deck of cards to play with because Brian's mother happened to mention that he liked to play Euchre.[45] After a couple of awkward minutes, Dale dealt the cards and they started to play.

Later, after everyone had left, Brian realized he was exhausted. He turned out the bright lights and crawled into bed, and started to think. Soon he began to realize how much he now appreciated Dale. Yes, Dale who had given him an amazing horse and a comfortable place to live. Brian appreciated those things. But Brian's true appreciation of Dale was for his real beauty—for the kind of person he was. In the short time that Brian

[45] Euchre: a card game played in the Midwest part of the United States

had known him, Dale made Brian feel welcome, like he had always been part of the family. Dale also had an easy laugh, and was patient with Brian when teaching him to care for horses. Plus, he didn't seem to have an office with Latin passwords required for entry. Dale continued to be nice to Brian no matter how rude Brian was to him. Although, Brian loved his dad despite his faults, he was realizing he could probably learn to love Dale, too. In fact, Brian now looked forward to getting to know Dale even better. With these new happy thoughts, Brian fell asleep easily.

The next morning, Brian went to the cafeteria by himself to eat. He was feeling a little lonely after seeing Bob's empty room. So, Brian returned back to his room—anxious[46] for Mum and Dale to come and take him home. He really wanted to groom Misty. Maybe she had calmed down and he could ride her, but he highly doubted it. Even if she had kicked him, it wasn't her fault. It was partially his fault for standing behind Misty and also partially due to the storm. However, it definitely wasn't Dale's fault, and Brian was particularly upset about how he had treated Dale.

While pondering [47] all of these thoughts, the doctor came in and asked if he could see Brian's head. Brian let him feel the bump and look at it.

"You are really healing remarkably[48] fast. You can go home today, okay?"

"Okay!"

[46] anxious: when you worry about something
[47] pondering: to spend time thinking about a situation or problem
[48] remarkably: to do something surprisingly well

Chapter 7:
Going Home

Brian tried to make time pass as quickly as possible until Dale and Mum arrived. Unfortunately, Brian felt an eagerness, which seemed to make time stand still and everything go slower. They were supposed to be there at noon, so he sat in his room glancing at the clock every five minutes—11:00, 11:05, 11:10 … 11:55 A.M.—*Five more minutes!* he thought.

Dale and Mum finally arrived at 12:26 P.M., late because the doctors had to talk to them about follow-up care. The nurse wheeled Brian out to Dale's car, and they headed home without a word.

When they got home and opened the door, Brian burst out, "I'm so sorry! I'm sorry, Dale. It's not your fault I had a concussion. I know it is my fault for being behind Misty."

"It's okay, Sonny. I forgive you. I'm

just so happy you are okay and that you are back here with us. Do you still want Misty?" asked Dale.

"Of course I do!"

"Then you'll be happy to know that she is fully trained and ready to ride!" he said, a wide grin spreading over his face.

"How could you train her in two days? You said it took months to train a wild horse," exclaimed Brian.

"Because she wasn't truly wild…she was rowdy, but not wild. She just had to calm down. Moving is hard for horses, too, you know," Dale said, winking. "She is outside, saddled in the pasture."

Brian ran outside, not caring how eager he appeared. In the pasture was

Zoe, holding Misty and Kit-Kat's reins in her hands.

"Want to ride?" she asked.

"You bet I do!"

"Then get your helmet on and let's go."

Brian put on his helmet, mounted Misty carefully, and nudged her gently.

Zoe opened the pasture gate and said, "Do you want to trot?"

"Sure," Brian said. Then he nudged Misty and she began to trot.

Brian bounced up and down with ease and comfort—without any fear. This beat any limo ride he had ever taken while living in New York City. All his life he thought cars were better than horses. Now he knew that the real beauty was in these majestic,[49] beautiful animals, and not in clunky metal cars.

Brian's far-off thoughts were then disturbed when Zoe shouted, "Hey, dreamer, try this." She lifted her leg up a little and nudged Kit-Kat in the side. Kit-Kat broke into a beautiful canter. "Go with the flow. Try to stay with your horse's motions or you'll fall."

So, Brian obediently[50] lifted his leg up and squeezed. Misty, too, sped into a canter as beautiful as Kit-Kat's. When he balanced his movements with Misty's, he felt like he was in the salty, blue-green ocean, swaying back and forth, the waves rising to the sun-baked shore

[49] majestic: extremely big and beautiful
[50] obediently: to do what you are told to do, to follow the rules

and then retreating again. Zoe didn't tell him to do this, but he nudged Misty again, and this time she broke into a full-out gallop. He lifted himself out of the seat of the saddle and leaned forward. He had never felt so free in all his life.

Zoe clapped as he pulled Misty back down to a walk. "That was beautiful!" she said in awe, "You are a natural."

They dismounted and walked Misty and Kit-Kat down to the stables. Then, they groomed and put saddle blankets on them before Zoe turned them out into the pasture to eat. Brian and Zoe walked back to their house, washed up, and went into the kitchen for dinner.

They ate, then Zoe asked, "Can

I show Brian his room?"

"Yes, go right ahead," Mum and Dale responded together.

"I know where my room is," said Brian confused.

"Yes, but you might not recognize it," Zoe said slyly.

When they walked in, he saw his furniture from New York City had been unpacked. His dresser, his books, his clothes, and even his small television.

"Cool!" Brian said.

"But that's not the best part," said Zoe. His walls had been painted green, as well as, new wallpaper that hung with horses running everywhere. They looked wild and free, just like horses should be.

Mum and Dale came in his new

room. "Do you like it?" asked Dale.

"Like it? I love it, Da-a-a-l ... Dad!"

Dale couldn't keep the heartfelt look of happiness from showing. "Before we go to bed," Dale began, "who wants to go for a drive around town in the truck? Maybe get some ice cream?"

Three "I do's" rang out, and everyone piled into the truck, for the first time, as a family.

*   *   *

Over the years, Brian and his step family became a real family. He visited his sister Carla and his Dad in New York City regularly. He was always glad to see them, but he loved to stay on the farm where he truly felt at home.

4114U

(Information For You!)

Written by:
Lynn Dubenko-Child/Family Psychologist,Ph.D
Kristyn Braund - 1st Grade Teacher
Billy Jack Blankenship - Religious Scholar
Colleen Ster - Research/Development/Illustrations

Kids: When your parents divorce or separate, you may feel like an earthquake has hit your family. The foundation that you have known since the day you were born is being shaken, stirred, and torn apart. You should know that the way you are feeling is very normal. The anger, hurt, frustration, and sadness that you are experiencing is part of the normal grieving cycle and the reason why you should keep talking to your parents. These feelings can be very overwhelming for an adult, but even harder for you to process. So just remember to keep communicating with family, friends, and especially with your parents as you go through these normal stages of grief.

We think of grief only being associated with death, but you can also grieve when you experience other types of losses in life. The stages that you may find yourself going though will include:

1. Denial: This can't be happening.
2. Anger: This is NOT fair!
3. Bargaining: It can work out.
4. Depression: Leave me alone.
5. Acceptance: Life is good again.

Parents: A parent's job is to give their children the tools they need to navigate, and to be active participants in solving problems that may come their way in life. Unfortunately, research shows that most children do not know or understand the reason for their parent's divorce; therefore, they assume that they are the problem or even the cause.

Please read through this 4114U section with your child. You will find helpful tips and activities for both of you. Hopefully, this book will open up a wonderful world of communication where you and your child can safely navigate through this tough situation together.

Action Steps to Help Kids Emotionally Through The 5 Stages of Grief

1. Denial
**This can't be happening to me.
Everything is fine.**

Express Yourself

After school, take some time to keep a journal of your thoughts and feelings from the day. Set a timer for fifteen minutes and make a commitment to experience and write your feelings instead of sitting in them all day.

You may notice a mixture of feelings:
- sadness
- anxiety
- anger
- relief

They are okay and normal, even if you feel them at the same time. It is important that you express these feelings, so you can get these thoughts and feelings out of your head and body.

This exercise can be exhausting, so make time to treat yourself after journaling. Relax and enjoy reading a good book, listening to music, seeing friends, and playing sports!

2. Anger
This is NOT fair! We are a family and must stick together.

It's Hot in Here!

Imagine you have a thermometer that measures how angry you feel. How do you know when you are warm, hot, or boiling with anger? At each temperature, ask yourself:

- How does my body feel (red face, clenched fists, tightened jaw)?
- What am I thinking about?
- How do I act (yell, throw things, cry)?

Learn how to recognize when you are just beginning to feel "warm" with anger and it will help you avoid the "boiling" point. When you start to feel "warm," try the belly breathing exercise below to help calm back down.

Blow off Some Steam

Many emotions, especially anger, can make our bodies uncomfortable. You may notice your heart beating faster, your muscles getting tighter, and your stomach feeling upset. Try this exercise to calm your body down and heal from the inside out:

Take a deep breath, all the way down to your belly, as if you are blowing up a balloon inside. Now, slowly let that breath out as you count to five. See how slowly you can breathe and how big your belly can get.

When you get even better at this breathing exercise, try blowing the biggest bubble you can, or see how long you can make a pinwheel spin. The trick is to use a long, slow, deep breath.

3. Bargaining
If I stop fighting with my sister and get better grades, then my parents will stop fighting and get back together.

It's Not Me, It's Them

You are not the one to blame for your parents' divorce or separation. Replace all those "If only I got better grades... If only I didn't fight so much with my brother/sister..." with the things that your friends and family love about you.

Try to write down ten things that make you a wonderful person. If you need help, ask others what they love about you.

✓ Check it off

If you notice that you are feeling sad, crying easily, losing energy, feeling overwhelmed, avoiding friends, and/or keeping to yourself, remember to "SMILE" every day:
- <u>S</u>ocialize
- <u>M</u>ove your body
- <u>I</u> Statements (I am strong. I am loved.)
- <u>L</u>augh
- <u>E</u>njoy something/someone

4. Depression
Everything is overwhelming to me.
I want to be left alone.

Puzzling

What may feel like a scattered life right now will certainly start to come back together for you. Imagine your life is like a puzzle. Which pieces of the puzzle do you need to feel settled in your life again? For example, the border of your puzzle may include your family and friends. The inside of the puzzle 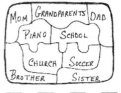 may include activities, sports, and school. Are there any pieces you would like to change, improve, replace, or add?

Enjoy the Ride

Any time you need a break, just close your eyes, take a deep breath, and go on a magic carpet or space shuttle ride. Pick any place you would like to be. You can go there any time, so notice all the smells, sounds, and sights. This is your happy place.

5. Acceptance

Maybe my parents and family will be happier living apart.

Comfy Cozy

If you are splitting time between your Mom's house and your Dad's house, make sure you have everything you need that makes you feel comfortable in both homes.  Do you have any special toys, photos, clothing, or blankets? Make a list of these things, and talk to your parents about having these items available at both homes.

Share the Love

You may feel like your family is being both torn apart and getting bigger at the same time. Your heart has an amazing way of growing to fit in everyone you love without taking love  away from anyone else. Draw your heart now, and then place a symbol for each person or thing you need to have space for inside your heart. Make sure you draw your heart big enough!

Action Steps To Help Families Socially

Kids: When going through a divorce or separation, you may feel like you are losing control and do not have any say over what is happening to your family. Keep a Grateful Journal and write three things you are grateful for everyday. Even in the midst of divorce, there are still things to be grateful for, like health, friends, and sunshine.

GRATEFUL JOURNAL

Journal Ideas:
- I really enjoyed Musical Theatre practice today. I don't know why, but when I am sad, I play the piano better and sing with more meaning. Music helps me to express how I am feeling and makes me feel better.
- I saw the most amazing rainbow today!
- This morning, it was a cold, winter morning and my Mom put my clothes in the dryer so they were nice and toasty when I got dressed!

Parent-to-Child Communication

Parents: When children feel like their foundation is crumbling, parents need to focus on creating structure, safety, and acceptance of the situation. Here are some suggestions to work through this process:

As in all experiences throughout life, communication is a key element, particularly between parents and children. This is especially true when trying to help your children understand divorce or separation. Just by opening the lines of communication with your children, you are allowing them to explore and understand why this is happening.

Helpful Tips:

• Communication Activities

Books and games are a wonderful way to open communication, particularly for younger children. Be creative and make up a game with long, thin stackable blocks where you write a question on each block that will help kids process life experiences. Stack the blocks, and then take turns pulling out one block at a time and answering the question written on each block.

Parents: The following book is a must read. According to *The Unexpected Legacy of Divorce: The 25 Year Landmark Study,* author Judith Wallerstein states that:

"The children have a right to know why their parents decided to divorce and what changes the divorce will set in motion. This is what they will take with them as they grow up, working and reworking every nuance of every message you send. At each developmental stage, children of divorce reassess their understanding of the divorce. They rehash it when they're grown and have children of their own and face their own crises. Conversation done fully and well will protect your child. If these discussions are done poorly or don't happen at all, the child is left to figure everything out on his own. Being left in the dark with a problem that is too big to understand increases a child's anxiety profoundly."

Wallerstein follows with the viewpoint of a child:

"[L]ike a child, you blamed yourself for the breakup. You must have done something bad to drive them [the parents] apart. You thought you were the most powerful villain responsible for the family disaster. If your parents were fighting over you and if you hadn't even been born, then they wouldn't have quarreled. You don't deserve to have good things happen. You certainly don't deserve to love or be loved."

This brings us to the next step. Have you sat down with your child and explained to them what contributed to the divorce? Your child is unaware of the reasons and may feel vulnerable and confused. Children have an egocentric "Me" mentality and will attempt to make sense of the divorce by blaming themselves. You can prevent that guilt and burden by providing them with specific, age-appropriate reasons.

What's to Blame

Children are used to discipline when bad behavior occurs; so, divorce to them feels like a punishment where someone/something is to blame. To illustrate the thoughts going through your child's head, take a look at the pie chart below and consider how much blame your child may be placing on themselves. If you can identify and eliminate any of these assumptions/thoughts, your child has a better chance to emerge from this experience feeling less confused, less vulnerable/scared, and more stable and confident.

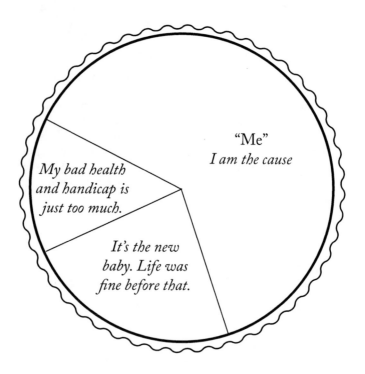

What's to Blame

Below is an exercise to help identify the real contributing factors that led to the divorce, and potentially provide conversation starters between you and your child. Remember that this is likely a conversation that your child(ren) will never forget, so choose your words lovingly, carefully, and try to remove any anger that you may be feeling.

Brainstorm additional ideas:

_____

_____

_____

_____

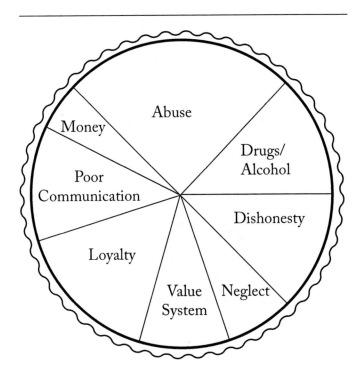

What's to Blame

Dear Parents and Children,

Please sit down and do this activity together. This is a unique moment for you and your child to realize that the divorce is not anyone's fault, but instead it is truly a combination of many factors.

Directions:

Below is an empty pie chart. The reasons for the divorce becomes the "filling" of the pie. By the time the filling is added to the pie, your child should have a better understanding of why the divorce occurred.

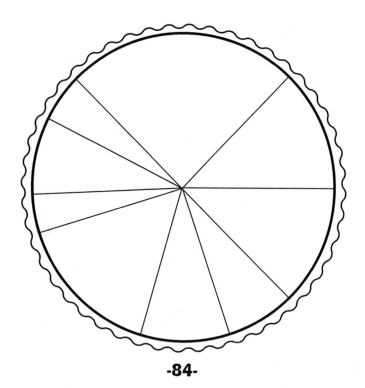

The Game Plan

While you and your child may feel less confused after identifying the factors that contributed to the divorce, you all are still probably experiencing many other confusing questions. As you move into the next step of creating a game plan together, here are some conversation starters to help you share your feelings with each other.

Parents:

Again, remember to choose your words carefully, as your child will likely remember this conversation for the rest of their life.

Parents: You probably have had some of these questions buzzing through your head:

- *How do I recover from this shattered family dream?*
- *How do I juggle being a parent alone?*
- *What is the plan for the future?*
- *I haven't worked in years. How am I going to support myself and my kids?*

Child Perspective: At the same time, your child will likely have some of the following ideas running through his or her head:

- *Where am I going to live?*
- *Do I have to switch to a new school?*
- *Can I keep playing on my sports team?*
- *Will there be money to pay for piano lessons?*
- *How can I be with my friends on the weekends?*
- *Do I now have to figure out a way to pay for college?*
- *Will I have to pay for my first car now?*
- *Will I live with my Mom or Dad? How about siblings?*

The Game Plan

Pretend you are in a basketball game: you have 30 seconds left on the clock with the game tied and your opponent has the ball. What is your next move? If you thought to call a time-out and come up with a game plan, then that is an excellent response. Just like you would create a game plan for a ball game, the same skills applies to everyday life. Sitting down with your child and creating a game plan together to maneuver through this divorce will help you to win in the end. So, even though this is an overwhelming time for all of you, stay positive, keep talking and create new strategies to make things work.

Sunday P.M.-Friday A.M.

- School homework
- Baseball practice
- Music lessons
- Friend play dates
- Youth Group
- Tutoring session

Friday P.M.-Sunday A.M.

- School homework
- Baseball games
- Music recitals/shows
- Hang with friends
- Friend parties
- House of Worship

Mom's House   Dad's House

Together

- Select holidays
- Teacher conferences
- Games, recitals, shows
- Child's birthday

Parent-to-Parent Communication

Parent-to-Parent communication is critical for teaching your children positive coping skills. Just remember, while divorce is a painful experience for everyone involved, it can also provide valuable lessons for your children. Use this opportunity to prepare them for future conflicts and difficulties.

Conflict Resolution

While you want to be honest with your children, keep adult conversations between the adults. Although it is a challenge, you must eliminate, or minimize sarcastic and negative comments about each other around the kids. It is inevitable that your children will witness a disagreement between their mom and dad.

If you find yourself arguing in front of the children, let them also see how you resolve the disagreement. This is a valuable opportunity for you to set an example of healthy expression and resolution. Your kids will learn effective communication skills that will benefit them throughout their lives.

However, if you feel the argument may escalate and that both parties are unable to resolve the disagreement amicably, then it is best to remove the child(ren) from the situation and continue the discussion in private.

Helpful Tips for Parents:

Discuss in advance what resources may be helpful to the children while they work through the divorce/separation. Consider what you both think will promote a healthy adjustment, including psychotherapy, school counseling, social events, and extra-curricular activities such as art, sports, dance and horseback riding. **Also, keep the rules the same between both houses. Children thrive in structure.**

You can even ask your children for their opinion so you can develop an understanding and an agreement as to what is most appropriate for them. Having this conversation when you are not in the heat of the moment will aid in the healing process for your child.

While it is common to talk with someone close to you or a therapist about the difficulties of divorce, this book illustrates how finding a meaningful "connection" with something can be therapeutic. Equine therapy has been shown to help increase self-awareness through a relationship with horses. The premise behind this therapy is that horses are social beings that rely on feelings, intuition, and instinct. Our relationship with them may allow us to disconnect from our rational mind and to reconnect with our emotions and body while giving us a "safe" relationship to explore trust and intimacy.

Parent-to-Teacher Communication

You must remember that the divorce is not just a "family affair." Your child will be taking their feelings from home and carrying them into their school day. As you all adjust to this new home life development, the kids will be conversing about this situation with their teachers and their friends.

Communicating with your child's teacher about what is happening on the home front will allow the teacher to be on the look out for red flags, such as incomplete in-class and at-home class work assignments, a drop in assessment scores, outbursts, or other attention-seeking behaviors.

Your child's teacher can be helpful by providing you with a list of friends for play dates. This can be a positive distraction. Your child's teacher knows the "school-version" of your child, which may be different than the "home-version" of your child. They are a wealth of information on how your child may really be feeling.

Remember that divorce or separation is not something you have to go through alone. Reach out to people who can be an added support system for your family and keep communication open with your family and friends. Alerting those who spend the most time with your child(ren), like family, friends, school teachers, and other caregivers, will help you resolve any difficulties much sooner. Ask these individuals to watch out for any warning signs in your child —> see next page.

What 2 Watch 4

Some red flags that indicate your child may not be handling the divorce as well as they are telling you would include:

- Incomplete Work
  - in-class/at-home assignments

- Attention-getting behavior
  - silliness, disrespectfulness, cursing, etc.

- Bed-wetting

- Attachment issues
  - crying when being dropped off at school, grandparents, child care, etc.

- Chronic Illness
  - stomach, head, muscle aches, etc.

- Withdrawal from friends, family, and hobbies/extra-curricular activities

- Anger Outbursts/Defiance

- Sleep Disturbances

- School Refusal

If you notice the warning signs above, please consider talking to your child about your concerns and then sharing them with a school counselor and/or psychologist to help your child resolve these issues more effectively.

Action Steps To Help Families Spiritually

When a person goes through a difficult time in life, they may often question their belief system or their house of worship. They may wonder why this bad thing is happening to them. According to Dr. Harold Koenig's book, *The Healing Power of Faith*, his research indicates that when people are faced with health problems or life challenges, it is the individuals with strong belief systems that have the best overall, positive recovery. When people can believe in something bigger than themselves, then they can heal faster and experience less pain.

Even though you feel like you are being torn between two new families and you feel the foundation beneath your feet trembling like an earthquake, you need to know that there is hope. Nobody—adult or child—is strong enough to go through a divorce alone. Having a strong connection with others, yourself, and a belief system can help you work through this difficult time and heal.

Helpful Tips:

Make sure you take time every day to reconnect with your belief system and detach yourself from concerns weighing you down. You can lift your spirits by dancing, praying, and singing. Immerse yourself in the comfort of your faith and let it protect you from discomfort and pain. Everyone needs some relief.

Affirmations:

Preserve your sense of confidence, worth, and self-esteem by writing a list of positive statements as a reminder that you are not defined by this divorce. By focusing on your strengths and who you want to become, you will feel the momentum that will push you directly through challenging and stressful life experiences—ultimately helping you heal.

You can hang this list in your locker, post it on your mirror, or write it in your journal.

Daily positive affirmations:

- I am not defined by divorce.
- I am a good student.
- I am a loyal friend.
- I am a creative writer.
- I like myself and who I am becoming.
- I have goals that I want to achieve.
- My dream is to be_____.

Spiritual Thoughts:

I turn over this painful situation to you because it is too big for me to deal with as a kid. Please give my family and me peace as we move through the healing process, and help me to accept change as it comes in my life.

In-depth 4114U

Written by: Billy Jack Blankenship, Religious Scholar
For an expanded version of this article, go to reflectionspublishing.com

Imagine an old, rusty bike. Restoring and fixing up that old bike does not mean throwing it away and getting a new one. It means that a person takes that old bike, scrapes off the rust, oils the gears, shines the frame, and puts air in the tires—he or she restores the bike. The old bike, with all the old parts, then becomes new. Just like the bike, we all have hurts that need to be healed and God is in the business of healing our pain and suffering.

Our parents' divorce happened because none of us are perfect. God hurts for those who have gone through the brokenness of divorce. It is very difficult to go through our parents divorce—the entire experience hurts. Sometimes we even lose trust in one or both of our parents and we feel like our life is in turmoil. We then question whether God is "out there" at all. Even though this situation hurts, there is hope. God did not plan for our parents to be divorced, and God didn't cause it to happen. Our parents chose that and even though our parents will probably never be together again, God is still at work, providing hope. God is healing our hurt and pain. God is concerned with who we are, and with our character and giving us faith and hope to help navigate through this tough situation.

"Dear Lord, I pray that my family will see blessings even in our difficult situation...as we seek to follow you, to serve you, to understand you and your story...and as we search for truth on this journey, even when we struggle, doubt, and wrestle with our faith in this difficult time. As we find ourselves in the deep and dark valley, I pray we will realize the darkness of that valley is only but a shadow—a shadow that is soon to be eclipsed by the light of the sun! And may that light guide us to the next mountain top."

About our Experts:

• Lynn M. Dubenko, Ph.D.

Dr. Lynn Dubenko, the founder of Vita Pondera Wellness,www.vitapondera.com, is a licensed clinical psychologist specializing in health psychology (PSY22882).

Dr. Dubenko's clinical experience and training include time at Pitt Memorial Hospital (North Carolina) and Rady Children's Hospital (San Diego), working with cardiac and pulmonary rehabilitation, pediatric hematology & oncology, and stress-related medical conditions. In addition, she has extensive experience working with children diagnosed with chronic pain and their families, treating a variety of conditions including migraine and tension headaches, abdominal pain, irritable bowel syndrome (IBS), fibromyalgia, chronic regional pain syndrome (CRPS), myofascial (muscular) pain, and injury-related pain.

In her private practice, Dr. Dubenko provides individual and group therapy for all ages, primarily using cognitive behavioral, mindfulness, and acceptance-based approaches to manage general stress, anxiety, and chronic illness. She also frequently uses biofeedback techniques, relaxation, and guided imagery. Lastly, Dr. Dubenko provides presurgical evaluations for those undergoing transplant, bariatric, or spinal surgeries.

Outside her practice, Dr. Dubenko enjoys mentoring doctoral students and spending time with her husband and two daughters.

About our Experts:

• Mrs. Kristyn Braund
Del Mar Union School District:
First Grade Teacher

Mrs. Kristyn Braund has been teaching first grade in the Del Mar Union School District for the past 5 years. Prior to that she taught Kindergarten in Oceano. Mrs. Braund received her B.S. in Liberal Studies as well as her teaching credential from California Polytechnic University in San Luis Obipso, CA. She is currently completing her Masters degree at San Diego State University.

• Billy Jack Blankenship
Solana Beach Presbyterian Church:
Associate Minister of Children,
Students, and Families

For over 10 years Billy Jack has served children/preteens in Southern California, at SBPC, and prior to that as the Director of Children's and Preteen Ministries at Forest Home Camps in the San Bernardino mountains. One of Billy Jack's true passions is using his own childhood divorce experience, and his own process of healing, to walk along side children with transparency and openness as they work through the divorce in their own families. "When a child realizes that I have also been through the difficulties of divorce, you can see the veil drop, and the child will begin to talk openly about his or her own experience which is a big step toward healing."

Children References:

- Brown, Marc and Laurene Krasney. *Dinosaur Divorce: A Guide for Changing Families*. New York: Little, Brown and Company, 1986.

- Gardner, Richard. *The Boys and Girls Book About Divorce*. New York: Bantam, 1985.

- Gray, Kes. *Mom and Dad Glue*. New York: Barron's Educational Series, 2009.

- Heegaard, Marge. *When Mom and Dad Separate: Children Can Learn to Cope with Grief from Divorce*. Minnesota: Woodland Press, 1990.

- Lansky, Vicki. *It's Not Your Fault, Koko Bear: A Read-Together Book for Parents and Young Children During Divorce*. Minnesota: Book Peddlers, 1998.

- Masural, Claire. *Two Homes*. Massachusetts: Candlewick Press, 2001.

- Longman English Dictionary Online - LDOCE, http://www.ldoceonline.com.

Adult References:

- Croasdale, Myrle. Body and soul: "When Faith Guides a Doctor's Vocation." *Amednews.com* published by American Medical Association. 24/31 December 2007. < http://www.ama-assn.org/amednews/2007/12/24/prsa1224.htm >

- Farber, Adele and Elaine Mazlish. *How to Talk So Kids Will Listen & Listen So Kids Will Talk*. New York: Harper Collins, 1980.

- Kluger, Jeffrey. "How Faith Can Heal." *Time 23* Febr. 2009.

- Koenig, Harold G, M.D. *The Healing Power of Faith: Science Explores Medicines Last Great Frontiers*. New York: Simon & Schuster, 1999.

- Kushner, Harold. *When Bad Things Happen to Good People*. New York: Avon Books - Imprint of HarperCollins, 1981.

- Wallerstein, Judith, with Julian M. Lewis and Sandra Blakeslee. *The Unexpected Legacy of Divorce: The 25 Year Landmark Study*. New York: Little, Brown and Company, 2000.

Book Club Discussion Questions:

1. Did it seem strange to you that Brian started calling Dale his Dad so quickly?

2. Have you ever moved or experienced a big, significant change in your life? If so, describe the emotions that you experienced.

3. List several ways that equine (horse) therapy can be therapeutic to children going through a difficult time.

4. Name several emotions that Brian probably felt as he was driving away from New York City and driving towards Wisconsin. Have you ever had to leave something you were comfortable with for something new?

5. Which characters in the story showed their "Real Beauty?"

6. What kind of parent do you want to be when you grow up?

7. Several communication techniques and activities are described in the back of this book. What was your favorite activity?

8. Have you ever had a strong connection with an animal like Misty or a person?

In-depth 4114U Concepts:

Page 3: Isolating patterns of behavior
Page 4: Internalizing feelings
Page 6: Loss = Grief
Page 7: Guilt: heavy weight of the world on kid's shoulders
Page 8: Change
Page 10: Anger: feeling "in the way"
Page 12: Distrust
Page 17: Scared: more change and adjustments
Page 20: Rejection
Page 30: Boundaries and Acceptance
Page 36: Grief
Page 52: Blame: divorce feels like getting kicked by a horse
Page 59: Friendship
Page 61: Appreciation

Acknowledgements

A wise, elementary principal once told me that our job as parents and educators is to teach our children the coping tools they need so when they find themselves in a difficult situation like getting bullied, going through a divorce, or experiencing peer pressure, then they will have these tools to access. This is the mission of Reflections Publishing——to allow children to help their peers through the power of their stories and illustrations and to allow experts to equip kids with the tools needed to survive in today's world.

This book would not have been possible without the numerous brainstorming and editing sessions with the following people. I thank you for your hours of dedication and passion to this mission.

Colleen C. Ster
President/Publisher of Reflections Publishing

Educators: Michelle Brashears, Kristyn Braund, Peg Conrad, Chris Delehanty, Kim Mowry, Sarah Raskin

Moms/Business Professionals: Lisa Aryan, Jamie Dicken, Beth Misak, Amy Mohr, Carol Ster, and Jennifer Tankersley

Child Psychologists/Family Therapists:
Karen Clark-San Diego Rescue Mission, FT trainee; Lynn Dubenko, Ph.D; Richard Griswold, Ph.D - School Psychologist AF/SC; Lewis Ribner, Ph.D; Linda Sorkin, MA, LMFT

Student Editorial Team: Savannah Cunningham, Juliette Dicken, Max Greenhalgh, Nicole Krakower, Kevin Misak, Mia Rogers, Caroline Ster, Megan Tankersley, Danielle Wood

CPSIA information can be obtained at www.ICGtesting.com
Printed in the USA
LVOW070537280512

283455LV00001B/27/P